Ca...
A Sto...   *...riends*

Author
Robert M. de la Torre
Born in Culver City, California 1958
Published by Author
Copyright 2009

Caterpillar Swing

On a good day, Charlie could do just about anything she put her heart to. She was an adorable creature full of life. Charlie was the envy of her peers, she was as smart as her teachers in any subject. Charlie, usually spent her time taking trips back and forth to the place she called the Swing.

There she would meet up with her friends, who were a lot like herself. The days would pass and Charlie would continue her trips to the Swing.

One day her life would change , it would become as though she was living in a dream.

A beautiful day had dawned and Charlie could hardly wait to greet the morning. She would finish her chores in record time, so she could meet up with her friends who would always wait for her.

Charlie usually wore her wooly sweater on days that were cold or looked as though it would rain. "It looks like rain today!" She would say. Her friends would always tell her, that it just looked that way, though Charlie always knew when it would rain.

On the way to the Swing , large clouds had started to form in the sky. Charlie looked up at the sky and waved her hands as if to say hello to the dark billowy clouds. Charlie would smile, and start to sing.

Her friends watched the drops of water falling from the sky from under a branch they were hiding under. There Charlie and her friends would spend the rest of the day, watching the rain fall and doing their best to stay dry.

"Charlie, Charlie, it stopped raining." Her friend said with a whisper. Charlie had fallen fast asleep while listening to the gentle rain. "The sound of rain always makes me sleepy." She said while rubbing her eyes.

It had stopped raining and Charlie and her friends were on their way to the Swing. The clouds had moved away and were moving away from them. Happy they were on their way, singing and holding hands.

At the Swing the friends would have the most enjoyable times together. There was lots to do and plenty of food to eat. Charlie's favorite food are blackberries and root grass. '

One time at the Swing Charlie and her friends ate so much, that they had turned the same color as the berries; dark blue.

It took them hours to get back home that day. Their stomachs were so full, they looked like they were going to pop. Charlie had warned them all not to eat too many berries. No one had paid any attention to her, but this time they did. The friends had all agreed to listen to

Charlie from that day on.

"We all better get home." Said Chello. "Wait until tommorrow, then we can come back here" Charlie had told them. She remembered that it was time for the journey back home. It took most of the day for Charlie and her friends to get to the Swing and most of the day to get back again. Charlie's legs were short and skinny and she had lots of them. Her legs moved so fast when she walked, you could hardly see them when they moved.

Chello could walk faster than Charlie, but he would always wait up for her. Chello looked out for her. It was Charlie who looked out for him, especially if she knew he would get into trouble.

So the friends started off on the journey back home. They were singing and holding hands like they did all the time.

All of a sudden, it was Charlie who saw a dark thing in the sky hovering over them. "What is that?" Asked Chello. The friends were looking up in the sky

and were frightened. "Look out!"
Charlie screamed. "Run and hide! She
commanded.

The friends scattered and ran for places
to hide. Charlie found a broken brick to
hide under. Chello saw a hole in the
ground and dashed into it. The other
friends had found places to hide also.
The sky began to get darker.

The darkness came down upon Charlie
while she was hiding under the brick. She
was unable to move out from underneath
it. Chello saw that she was helpless and
called the friends to come and help him.
The friends all helped Chello move the
brick and Charlie was free again.

One of the youngest friends asked
Charlie what that dark thing was and
she told her that it was a shoe. "Wow,
you were sure lucky Charlie!" Said the
youngest friend. Charlie smiled and told
the youngest that if she ever saw that
again, to go run and hide. Chello said
that he had enough excitement for one

day and wanted to go home.

Tossing and turning all night, Chello was having a bad dream. He remembered the dark thing coming down upon them. He woke up dizzy and shaking. Chello thought to himself that they sure had a close call from the shoe. Charlie told him about the dark thing before but he forgot all about it. He was glad to have a friend like Charlie, who always helped him out when things went bad.

"Hello, Hello!" It was Charlie calling out to Chello. She could see that he had a bad dream again. "How many times do I have to tell you?" She scolded. Chello looked at her puzzled and then she said that it was just a dream.

Charlie just laughed at him and began to tell Chello about the dream she always has. It was most of the day that Charlie would amuse Chello with her stories about her dream. He would just sit there listening to her go on and on about it. She tells him that they both would no longer have to live the way they do on the ground anymore. Chello sometimes thinks to himself that Charlie is crazy.

"You mean we won't be the same anymore?" Asked Chello. "Yes, that's right Chello" Answered Charlie. She tells him how the two of them will live up above. Then she tells him how they will look different. '

Chello sometimes thinks to himself that Charlie is crazy. He doesn't like to see her get angry, so he listens to her with a smile.

"Are we going to the Swing today?" Chello asks. "No, today we going to go to a place to see something new" She tells him. "Like where?" He inquires. "It's a surprise, just follow me." Was her answer.

The two set went off, singing and holding hands like they always did. Charlie wanted to show Chello a place that reminded her of her dream. The two

spent most of the day walking.
They arrived to this place and there was lots of things to do. Chello had never seen anything like it before.

"What's that?" Asks Chello. "That's a bird." Answers Charlie. Much like the shoe, Charlie warns Chello of danger and to be very careful.
"Don't let him see you, we are his favorite food" she tells him. Chello ducks down as if he had been seen by the bird and starts to tremble.

"It's ok, he can't see us if we stay on this leaf, he doesn't know we're here. Chello looks at Charlie feeling more confident that he won't become the bird's lunch. "I want to show you something else." Says Charlie. "It's ok, I've seen enough for one day and want to go home now" Chello cries. "Don't be silly, we have lots to do today and I need you to be brave." She tells him.

Charlie and Chello come to a new thing that he has never seen before. He finds

himself looking into a pond of water.
Chello feeling better now that the bird is
forgotten, starts to touch the water. He
sees the ripples that he made and starts
to sing. The two look down into the
pond and see their own reflection. Chello
starts to laugh at the way the ripples
make him look funny.

Charlie sees a falling leaf from a tree
and tells Chello to give her a hand.
"What are we going to do with that?"
Asks Chello. "We are going to make a
boat." Answers Charlie. Chello looks at
her with a puzzled look on his face.
"Help me push it into the water Chello."
She asks him.

The huge leaf floats close to the edge of
the pond and Charlie yells to Chello to
"Get on!"
Chello hops up onto the leaf boat and
yells out loud with glee. "We're moving
Charlie" He says. Charlie is smiling
from ear to ear as they start to drift
away from the edge of the pond.

The two friends are once again on another journey, not knowing what waits ahead of them.

The leaf boat far from the edge of the pond, starts to take on water. Chello looks at Charlie and starts to get frightened. The both see the other side of the pond and Charlie tells him to paddle. "Chello, get ready to jump off." Says Charlie. The leaf boat comes to rest at the edge of the pond, and both of them jump off the leaf boat.

Charlie shouts out loud, "Here we are!" The leaf boat slowly starts to disappear into the water. "Wow, we got off just in time." Says Chello. Charlie smiles and tells him that is why you always pick a large leaf to make a boat with.

Once the two arrived at the other side, they both start walking to a place that Chello has never seen before. Everything was quite different from where he had come from. It was Charlie that knew the place well, she had spent lots of time *there, and think about the change that she would have. She knew that the time would come soon.*

"Chello come over here, I want to show you something." Said Charlie. Chello ran over to where she was and looked to see what it was she wanted him to see. "Look over there!" She pointed up. Chello saw her staring up to the clouds with her mouth open. In the distance was a huge rainbow. "Wow, that is so pretty!" Remarked Chello. The colors were beautiful and Charlie started to sing. The two friends looked at each other and began to dance. The rainbow glistened bright with all it's radiant colors. It stayed in the sky for awhile then it started to rain.

"We better get started home Chello." Said Charlie. "Let it rain, I don't care." Replied Chello. The sight of the rainbow made his whole day. The two agree to get on their way to make the journey home. The two decided to wak instead of

taking the leaf boat. Besides, it was raining and didn't want to take a chance on sinking in the middle of the pond.

It was getting dusk and the two hurried to get back home. At home they could get dry and have some leaf tea then rest up.

The two sat next to each other resting their tired legs. It had been a long day and both of them were exhausted from the walk back home.

Sipping their tea they had talked about the rainbow and the leaf boat the Chello had never seen before. Chello kept talking about how the leaf boat almost sank into the pond. Charlie smiled at him as she rested up and was glad he got to ride the leaf boat for the first time.

After a long story about her dream, Chello had fallen asleep. She finished her tea and covered Chello, then kissed him goodnight. "Goodnight Chello" she whispered. Chello had a smile on his face and rolled over.

The sun was baking down upon them

when they woke up. Charlie was wiping the sleep from her eyes and noticed Chello was still sleeping. She put some water on for some leaf tea and greeted the day with a smile.

The sun was too hot that morning and Charlie knew that they would have to find shade. Her skin was too fair for the heat and it made her sick. Chello appeared out from under his leaf and Charlie asked him if he was awake. "I think I'm awake now" He said. "Come on over here and have some tea, we have to get started you know." She told him. "Today will be hot and we must find shade." She said . Chello picked himself up and sipped his leaf tea before she could say anything else.

Some of the friends had been waiting outside for the two, so they could all go searching for shade to stay in for the day. The sun was beating down hard and they had to get started right away.

Charie and Chello soon made their

morning appearance. One of the friends asked them if they had slept good. "I slept fine." Replied Charlie. "Me too." Was Chello's reply. They all began their search for shade.

Charlie gave Chello a leaf and told him to put it on his head. Chello took the leaf and covered himself with it. He could see that Charlie had already put hers on. The friends all had their leaf hats and on their way they went to look for shade. They were all singing and holding hands.

"Look!" Chello shouted. "What is it Chello?" Asked one of the friends. "I see something over there!" He cried out. All of the friends turned their heads to see where he was pointing, they saw a deep hole in the side of a hill.

"Charlie come and see!" He shouted to her. "Oh dear." She sighed. "It's a nice place for the day, we all can stay here, away from the sun." She said. Chello was proud of himself, that he was the first to spot a nice place that they all could stay in.

At first they were all uncertain of the place and approached it with caution. Charlie moved closer and closer to the entrance of the place. She told everyone not to be afraid. "It looks dark in here." Chello mentioned. Charlie assured everyone that it was ok to go inside.

Chello started his way in and the friends were right behind him. "Wow, it sure is dark in here" Chello announced. "Don't worry your eyes will adjust, it just takes a few moments." Assured Charlie. The friends all stayed close to each other once they all were inside. Charlie told them all again that it would be soon before they could see.

"I can see now!" Announced Chello. "Me too!" Said one of the friends. "It's nice and cool in here." Remarked Charlie. Charlie and the friends began to explore the place and go further in the opening. Staying close together and still holding hands, they went deeper and deeper into the place. The coolness of the walls, with moisture dripping down from the ceiling offered a great place to stay for the day.

Chello had gone further into the place on his own, not taking notice that the friend were out of view. He saw some roots hanging down from the ceiling and became curious. Chello started pulling at the roots and noticed sap dripping off of them. He tasted the sap and it reminded him of berries that grew from the Swing.

All of a sudden he became delighted from its delicious flavor and he became so happy to tell everyone what he had found. "Wait Chello, don't do anything until we all get there!" She commanded. The friends hurried over to see what Chello had found. Charlie was shocked to see what he was doing. "Stop, be careful not to disturb those roots!" She shouted.

It was too late, he had wiggled them enough to disturb the tiny creatures that lived in them. The friends were standing there in awe, while a few tiny heads began to appear from the cracks in the roots. One by one and two by two, they cold see the tiny heads appear until there were hundreds of them.

"Wow, unbelievable!" He screamed. Charlie shouted over to Chello and told him to get back. Still holding the root in his hand he slowly moved away from where the tiny creatures had appeared.

"What are those Charlie?" One of the friends asked her. "Those are ants?" She replied. They all stared at the tiny creatures with amazement.

"Wow!" one of the friends shouted. By then the tiny head grew in numbers and were multiplying. The curious creatures had moved out from the cracks and were surrounding the friends. Charlie told everyone to stay close together and not to be frightened.

Chello was shaking and moved closer to Charlie. He looked up at her and she

smiled at him. Being surrounded by the
many creatures with no plans for escape,
they all huddled close to each other.

  A loud voice was heard and asked,
"What do you think your doin here?"
Charlie and the friends knew the question
was directed to them and moved closer to
each other. "What do we tell him?"
Asked Chello. "We came here in search of
some shade." Was her reply. "Shade,
what do you mean shade?" Asked the
loud one.

Charlie told him that they meant no
harm and they would leave right away.
The loud one was staring into her face
with an angry look about him. "We
promise to leave right now" Charlie told
him. "Yes of course you will, but first I
want you to come back and bring us some
food." He explained. "Ok, we will if you
promise to let us go now." She replied.

  Charlie's calmness had paid off, she and
the friends began to leave the place.
Hundreds of tiny heads that were staring

at them all started to go back into the cracks. The last one to leave was the loud one, who told them what would happen if they didn't make good their promise.

Moving out from the place the friends were all glad that nothing went wrong. They were on their way home again. Charlie wasn't too mad at Chello for disturbing the roots. She told him that he would be the one to pick the food for the ants. Chello agreed, and told Charlie that he was sorry for what he had done. She smiled at him and said not to worry, that everything was ok. That night when Charlie and the friends had arrived home they all took turns telling their story about the place. For some of the friends it was their first encounter with the creatures. "Did you see the one with the beedy eyes?" Chello asked them. "He didn't scare me!" boasted the oldest friend. Charlie giggled while looking at their faces, seeing how serious they were

as they told each other their stories and
described the ants.

Chello said he wasn't afraid while
moving closer to Charlie. "Why were
you shaking then?" she asked him.
Chello's face was blushing and she
pushed him away. The friends all looked
at Chello and started laughing. Then the
all smiled at him said that he was the
bravest. Chello's face lit up and he stood
up high and proud.

It was getting late and Charlie was the
first to turn in for the night. Chello and
the friends went to pick their leaf beds so
they all could get some sleep. Charlie
bidded them all a goodnight and turned
over and closed her eyes. Chello and the
friends all did the same.

The next morning the sun was shining
down on the leaf hut. A few billowy
clouds were floating by and it looked like
it was going to be a good day. Stretching
out her arms, Charlie went out to greet
the day. Chello and the friends were soon

awake while Charlie started making leaf tea for them all.

"Chello, as soon as you wake up, go and gather food for the ants!" She told him. Chello sipped his tea and finished it, then went out to gather the food. The friends were not about to let Chello go by himself, so they all agreed to go with him.

"Let's go and get the food at the Swing" Charlie said. She told them it was on the way to the place and they all had agreed while Chello told them that he was getting hungry with all the talk of food. "We'll get berries, they will like berries." Mentioned Charlie. They all had agreed to bring berries to the ants.

While picking berries at the Swing, the friends did'nt know that the ants were in their place and had become sick. As soon as the friends arrive to the place they noticed that the roots weren't hanging down from the ceiling like before.

"Charlie look at this, all the roots are

gone now" Chello reported. "Isn't that strange" replied Charlie. "I wonder what happened here, and why the ants have not come out to greet us?" She asked puzzled. "Let's take the berries and leave this place." Said Chello. The friends all agreed and started to move out from the place.

Charlie was feeling funny about the whole thing.

"Chello, what's that you have there?" She asked him. "I don't know, I found it over there!" He pointed. Charlie saw that it was a note. It was a clue to what had happened. Charlie was the only one who could read out of all of them. She read the note out loud. "To the honest ones who came to bring us food, we thank you all".

Charlie wasn't satisfied with the note, she knew there was something more. "Chello come and bring me some berries" she told him. She took some berries and placed them by the cracks then moved

away. In a moment a tiny head
appeared, it was the loud one. "We have
the foood you wanted" Said Charlie.
"Ok, just leave it and go!" Barked the
loud one.
  He wasn't so loud that time and he
looked pale.
Charlie thought to herself that he was
ill. Charlile asked if everything was ok
and climbed back down. She had figured
out why all the ants had not appeared,
they must have eaten all the roots and
sap and got sick. They all left the food
for the ants, then went off again.
  "Where are we going now?" Asked one
of the friends. "Let's all go have some
fun!" Was Charlie's reply. They all
agreed to go and have some fun. This
time Charlie suggested they take the path
to the Swing with the stick bridge on it.
When they arrived at the stick bridge,
Chello wanted to cross first. Charlie and
the friends let Chello go first, they
remembered how he liked to be first. He

started his way onto the stick bridge and when he got to the middle and it started to wobble.

Charlie saw the Chello was having trouble by the way the stick bridge was swaying back and forth. "Help! Help! I'm losing my balance!" He shouted. Charlie and the friends could not get to Chello to help him. They all stood there watching him sway back and forth. Chello was screaming louder, "Help me!"

Charlie felt helpless as she tried to figure out how to help Chello. She told her friends to hurry and get under the stick bridge and start piling up leaves for Chello's fall. Chello had already started to fall. "Get ready to catch him!" she yelled. The friends were under the stick bridge waiting for him to fall into the leaves they had piled up. "Yeowww!" Chello screamed as he came crashing down.

"That was fun, let's do it again!" He shouted. Chello was smiling from ear to ear. Charlie started to laugh out loud. One minute Chello was scared silly and the next he was happy as can be.

The friends piled up more leaves under the stick bridge. Chello had started something new for them to do that day. They all decided to draw straws to see who would go next. The youngest friend drew a long straw and everyone else had drawn a short straw. She got to go next. She crawled up to the stick bridge and started to get to the middle when it had started wobbling.

All the friends were cheering her on. "Whaaa!" She screamed. She was on her way down, falling fast into the pile of leaves waiting for her. She crashed into the leaves and disappeared. Her head popped up and they all started laughing and dancing.

She brushed herself off and caught her breath while Chello and the others started piling up more leaves.

Charlie climbed up to the stick bridge

with a big smile on her face. She went out to the middle and it began to wobble just like it did with the others. Back and forth she began to swing, until she had lost her balance. "Yahoo!" she yelled out. Falling fast she began to tumble down into the big pile of leaves. With a huge smile on her face she popped up from under the leaves. The friends all started dancing and singing.

For the rest of the day Charlie and the friends took turns falling from the stick bridge. They had so much fun that they didn't realize it was getting late.

The sun was going down, so the friends decided to head back home. They were all exhausted from having so much fun. "Let's come back again tommorrow!" cried Chello. They all started laughing at him, he had a leaf sticking out from the top of his head.

That night Charlie and Chello were sipping their leaf tea before bed. Chello asked her to tell him about her dream.

She took a sip of tea and smiled at him and agreed to tell him the dream.

Chello got comfortable on his leaf and sipped tea while Charlie began to tell him of a time when things would change for them. She told them about how they would no longer live the way they do. Chello listened with stars in his eyes when she told him how they would live in the sky. Chello would giggle every now and then to let Charlie know that he was happy.

Chello's eyes began to droop as she went on with her dream. He had fallen fast asleep before she could finish her story. Charlie took a leaf and covered him, then took a sip of leaf tea and went to sleep herself.

"Hello, is there anybody home?" Asked the oldest friend. He had been awake most of the night and wanted to talk to Charlie. When she woke up and saw him there, she noticed he looked very tired. "Can I get you something?" She asked

him. "No, I have already had some tea."
He said. "Charlie, I have to talk to you,
it's important." He stated. "Ok let me
get ready, I'll be with you soon." She
told him. Charlie was usually the one
the friends would talk to when there was
a problem. She was thinking to herself
what he wanted and if everything was
ok.

The oldest friend began to tell her about
the change he saw, that Charlie always
talked about. Charlie became very
interested in his story and thought how
similar it was to her dream. The friend
told her that it happens to all of them.
Charlie told him that he should not talk
about it yet to the others. The oldest
friend promised he wouldn't.

Charlie asked him when the change
happens and he told her that he wasn't
sure. He did tell her that he noticed his
skin had turned a dark color. The oldest
friend went off that day and he never
returned .

Charlie was thinking to herself that one day she too would start to change and have to go off somewhere. Charlie smiled and knew that the change would be good. She wouldn't let it bother her too much to think about it.

"Charlie, Charlie what were you two talking about?" Asked Chello. "Oh it was nothing, we were just talking." She told him. Chello didn't ask Charlie too many questions after that and went on with what he was doing.

"Where are the others?" Asked Charlie. "They went off to the Swing." He mentioned. "Why didn't you go with them?" She inquired. "Oh, I thought maybe just me and you would go by ourselves." He told her. "Chello, I want you to know that it's just a dream." She assured him. "Oh, I'm not thinking about that." He said. Charlie didn't want Chello to get worried about it. She told herself that for the rest of the time together she would keep it to herself.

By the time the friends returned from gathering food, Charlie and Chello had already left for the Swing. Holding hands and singing, they were off on another adventure. The two were quite a pair. Just like they were meant for each other. Charlie being the smart one and full of energy. Chello being the brave one, always finding trouble.

The two came upon the Swing, they had arrived there in record time. "Charlie, what do you say we climb a tree today?" She asked him. Charlie knew she had her hands full and wondered what on earth he wanted to climb a tree for.

Chello had remembered when he saw the bird for the first time. "Chello, do you want to make the bird mad at us?" She asked him. Chello took some leaves and put them all over himself.

He told Charlie to do the same thing. She looked at Chello as if he were crazy, then put the leaves all over herself. "He won't see us like this." He said proudly.

Charlie started laughing and went along with his idea.

All covered up in the leaves the two started to luagh at each other. "You look funny Chello" Charlie told him. "You ought to see yourself Charlie." He said to her. The two of them looked up at the big tree and started to climb up high. "Make sure you don't make any noise." She said in a whisper. "Ok I promise" He replied.

The two climbed higher and higher, then they spotted a dark hole in the tree. Chello couldn't help it, he had to take a look inside. Chello stuck his head into the dark hole and started to pull himself up further into it. Chello went too far and had slipped in the dark hole.

Charlie's heart started pounding and saw only his feet sticking out from the hole. She pulled his feet as hard as she could and Chello started to come out. She finally got him out, then Chello looked at her and she thought he was going to faint.

Charlie asked Chello if he was ok, he told her that he was fine. "Let's get going, we've had enough." Said Charlie. "What did you see in the dark hole Chello?" She asked him. "It was terrible." He said. "It was the bird, he was asleep." He told her. Charlie told him that he was very lucky that he didn't wake up the bird.

"Let's just forget it." He said to her. "Ok Chello, we won't talk about it." She assured him. Charlie had to look away so Chello wouldn't see her laughing.

The two took off walking away from the big tree and talked about what they wanted to do next. The day was still young, and there was still plenty to do.

Chello was getting hungry from all the excitement and so was Charlie. They both decided to find some food and take a break for awhile. "Charlie, let's have a picnic!" He shouted. "Ok, that sounds like a good idea to me Chello." She answered.

The two gathered berries and leaves, then Charlie found two big ones and made a sun cover. They sat underneath it and started to eat their lunch. It was a beautiful picnic, the two ate their berries and drank tea and talked about the climb up to the dark hole and laughed at how Chello became stuck in it.

"You should have seen the look on your face when you got out of that hole" Charlie said smiling. Chello laughed at Charlie as she made a face. Charlie would always ask herself what she would do without Chello. For sure her life would be dull and meaningless. The two finished their picnic and started their way back home.

When they were about half way back home they noticed the ants were marching along the side of the path. Chello moved closer to Charlie and asked her what they were doing. She wasn't quite sure herself and told Chello to move out of the way as they marched on by.

One of the ants looked over at Charlie then he turned back again. "Where are you going?" She asked the ant. The ant looked straight ahead, then turned back again and said that they were moving to their new home. "We must find food!" He told her.

Charlie noticed the ants were marching straight for the Swing. She told Chello that if the ants found the berries they would eat them all and not leave any. Charlie remembered the stick bridge that lead to the entrance of the Swing. She told Chello to hurry and follow her to the shortcut there. The two hurried off to the stick bridge and got there before the marching ants.

"Chello helped Charlie move the stick bridge away from the pond so the marching ants would not be able to cross into the Swing. Both of them moved the stick bridge to the edge of the pond and pushed it far from the edge of the pond.

Charlie and Chello looked for a place to

hide so the ants wouldn't see what they had done. The leader of the ants saw that it was no use to get to the other side and shouted, "Follow me!" The marching ants all went on another path away from the Swing.

Charlie had decided that they had enough for one day and they started their way back home.

Chello could hardly wait to get there so he could tell the friends how he save the berries from the marching ants.

The friends were all happy that the berries didn't get eaten up by the ants. They had remembered how they ate all the roots in the place. Charlie told them all that it was Chello who save the berries. Chello refused to take the credit by himself and said that it was Charlie who had the idea.

Night was falling and they were all tired from gathering food. It was a warm night out and they all decided to camp out under the stars. Charlie was busy

making some leaf tea for the evening.
The friends looked for leaves so they
could make their beds. "Look at all the
stars" said Chello. "Aren't they
beautiful" Charlie replied. "I wonder
how many there are?" Asked the
youngest friend. "Who knows, there has
to be a zillion." Remarked Chello.

Charlie was staring out into the night
looking for shooting stars. "What's that
Charlie?" Asked the youngest friend.
Charlie pointed up and told her it was a
shooting star. Charlie and the friends
were amazed by its brilliant light and
long tail that it left behind.

They were all sipping their tea, telling
stories to one another. The night was
long and they were all getting tired. One
by one they dozed off beneath the
blackened starry sky. Charlie still awake
began to hum a song, smiling that the
day had been good. She soon became
sleepy and took one last sip of her leaf
tea and made her bed.

The morning came fast for Charlie and her friends. They all woke up fresh and started telling each other about their dreams. Chello didn't bother to ask Charlie about hers, he already had a good idea what hers was about.

"What did you dream about last night, Chello?" Asked one of the friends. "Me, I drempt about the shooting stars." Was his answer. "Oh, tell us please, we want to know!" Cried the youngest. Chello began to tell them about his shooting star dream. He began by saying how he rode one all the way across the sky. Charlie couldn't help laughing. She had to turn her head away so Chello wouldn't see her face. Chello looked over at Charlie with a puzzled look on his face, then started to finish his story. "Then I rode it all the way as far as the moon." The friends couldn't help it anymore, they all started laughing at Chello with the most serious look on his face.

Charlie had to leave the place where they were sitting. Chello became embarrassed at the friends laughter and stopped his story. Charlie came back to where they were sitting and told Chello to go ahead and finish his story. He sat down on his leaf and said that he was finished anyway. He sunk his head down, then lifted it back up again and gazed out in to the sky.

Chello then got up from his leaf and started wandering off. "Where are you going?" Charlie asked him. "I'm going to go for a walk, I'll be back soon" He replied. The friends didn't want Chello to leave, neither did Charlie. They all circled around Chello so he couldn't get away. Then they all started singing and dancing. Chello looked for an opening but it was no use. They had made him dizzy and he couldn't keep himself up. Chello did a few twirls then fell to the ground.

Charlie could see that he had enough of

the circle game by the way he tried to focus. "It's my turn!" Shouted the youngest. The friends put the youngest in the circle and started singing and dancing. She started twirling and finally got dizzy, then fell to the ground. Charlie picked her up and dusted her off, then she went to sit down.

"Ok, my turn!" Shouted another friend. Everyone took turns inside the circle until it was Charlie's turn. All the friends took her to the circle and began to chant "Charlie, Charlie, Charlie. She began to twirl around and around while the friends circled her. Charlie then started getting dizzy and was loosing her balance. She lost focus and fell to the ground.

Chello noticed that Charlie wasn't smiling or too happy and ran over to her. "Are you ok Charlie?" He asked her. "I'm ok, I think." She replied. All the friends helped Chello take her to a leaf where she could rest.

"I'm ok Chello, please go and get me some tea." She asked him. Chello went off quickly to get her tea while the friends looked after her. "I feel something strange in my side." She said with a sigh. "What is wrong Charlie?" They asked her.

"I don't know, I never felt like this before." Was her reply. Chello came back with the leaf tea and was glad she was sitting up. "Don't worry Chello I'll be ok." She told him.

The friends were glad to see that Charlie was ok and went to find their leaves for the evening.

Charlie and Chello stayed up that night talking about the circle game. Chello made sure that she was comfortable and had plenty of leaf tea.

The two agreed that they would not go to the circle anymore. Chello had a lot of concern for his friend Charlie. He layed on his leaf looking up to the sky. Charlie was humming her favorite song while sipping her tea. She looked over at Chello and smiled and said to herself that she was lucky to have a friend like him.

That afternoon Charlie and Chello just stayed in the leaf hut while the friends were out playing. They could hear singing and chanting as they continued with the circle game. Charlie told Chello that she was feeling better then got up to make more of the leaf tea.

Chello had already fallen asleep by the time Charlie came back. Charlie went outside to join the friends who were happy to see her and that she was doing fine. "I never had this pain in my side before." She said with concern. The oldest friend asked her what it felt like, then noticed a small bump where she was holding it. Charlie moved her hand away and saw that it was moving. Charlie put her hand back to hide the bump.

"We must not tell Chello." She said. "We won't tell him." They promised her.

The next day when Charlie woke up she noticed that the bump had gone away. Chello had a good nights sleep and was happy to see that Charlie was doing good. "Would you like something to eat Chello?" She asked him. Chello told her that he was famished, while rubbing his belly. Charlie went over to the basket and pulled out two big berries for Chello. He looked at her and was smiling. They both ate their breakfast before they went outside.

"Chello, what do you say we go for a nice walk today?" She asked him. "That's a great idea." He replied. He started getting ready for the walk to the Swing. The two started walking on their way to the Swing and saw the friends playing. "Where are you going off to this time?" They asked. Chello yelled back at the friends and told them that they were off to the Swing.

The friends joined Charlie and Chello for a walk to the Swing. They all started to sing, while holding hands as they danced off. By the time they had come to the entrance to the Swing, all the friends agreed to stop and rest for ahwile. Chello still wanted to continue on, then Charlie told him to stop and take a break. He found himself a rock to sit on and held his head down. "Cheer up Chello, we will get there soon enough." They told him. Chello raised his head up and so everyone would see that he wasn't unhappy.

From nowhere the darkness appeared and the friends ran to find places to hide. Chello was right behind them all but didn't notice if Chello was with them. The darkness was coming down fast. Chello looked up and saw that it had fallen upon him. "Help! Help!" He screamed. It was too late, the darkness was not a shoe this time, it was the bird.

The bird had seen Chello by himself and swooped down and scooped him up with his long beek. "Owwwww! Help!" He screamed again. The friends and Charlie had seen the bird scoop up Chello and were running in circles trying to think of what to do to help poor Chello. Charlie was shocked to see her friend taken away to the sky by the big bird.

The bird was flying around in circles trying to find a place to land so he could make a meal out of Chello. Charlie saw that he wasn't hurt by the powerfull bird. She noticed his legs were still kicking furiously. All of a sudden the big bird let out a cry, "CaCaw!" It cried. The big bird had let Chello free from it's strong beek and Chello came falling back toward the ground. The friends that were looking on became delighted to see that Chello didn't get eaten by the big bird.

Charlie's heart was pounding as she started running toward where Chello fell. With a "Thump!" Chello hit the ground. He saw Charlie running toward him and yelled out, "I'm ok!" Charlie saw that Chello only had a bruise where the big birds' beek had him. "Chello, are you hurt anywhere?" She asked him. "No, I'm fine just a bit nervous." He replied. Charlie smiled at him and the friends had picked him up and took him to a place where he could rest awhile.

"I tickled his tongue!" Shouted Chello. "What do you mean Chello?" She asked. "I was tickling the big birds tongue, so he would let go of me." He said smiling. Charlie couldn't believe what he had said and started laughing. All the friends started laughing with her. Chello was proud of himself and laughed along with them.

After a few moments Chello was ready to go on ahead to the Swing. They all took off singing and dancing while holding hands. The youngest friend told Chello that he was her hero. Chello smiled at her and felt proud of what he had done.

"Good job Chello, glad your'e still with us." Said the oldest. "Glad to be with you." He said in return.

At the Swing the friends all decided to visit the pond. Chello was getting hungry from all the excitement and started picking berries.

Out from under the shrubs where he was picking berries, a small green head appeared to him. "Hey what are you going to do with those berries?" He asked Chello. Chello didn't see who was talking to him, the shrubs were the same color as the green head that popped out. Chello yelled out, "Hey these shrubs are starting to talk." Charlie looked over at him and told him to be careful of the snakes. "What snakes?" Chello asked. "I'm a snake." Said the green headed creature. The snake wiggled up close to Chello and asked him, "So, you have never seen a snake before?" "No, I can't say I have." Replied Chello. "Do you have a name?" Asked the snake. "Yes, my name is Chello." He answered. "My name is Theodore." Said the snake.

"Nice to meet you." Returned Chello. Chello noticed that he didn't have a hand to shake.

They both looked each other over and Theodore went back into the shrubs. "Bye!" Said Chello waiving his hand. Charlie went over to where Chello was standing and gave him the basket so he could fill it with berries. "Did you make a friend Chello?" She had asked him. Chello told her that they just met and the snake didn't say anything about friends. "Did he say if he was coming back?" She asked him. "No, he just disappeared into the shrubs. "That's odd." Remarked Charlie.

The friends were at the pond and they had all made leaf boats. Charlie asked Chello if he remembered how to make one. Chello nodded his head and started looking for a nice size leaf to make his boat with.
Charlie helped Chello pick out a big one, so they could put it in the pond.

The leaf boat was floating close to the edge of the pond and Charlie jumped up onto the boat first, then Chello. "Hurry let's catch up with them!" Shouted Chello. Charlie noticed that the friends were getting too close to the falls and started yelling at them to watch out. The friends were too far to hear what Charlie had said to them. They were heading for the falls fast.

Theodore heard what was going on and slipped into the pond. The friends saw that they were heading for the falls and started yelling. They tried to turn the leaf boat around but it was no use, the current was too strong. "Help, Help!" They cried.

Theodore saw that if he could stretch himself out over the pond, he could stop the leaf boat from going over the falls. Charlie and Chello were amazed to see what Theodore had done. The leaf boat was stopped by his long body and they were saved from going over the falls.

"Get on my back and I'll take you to shore" he told them. The friends climbed on top of his back and then Theodore swam to the edge of the pond. "Hurray for Theodore!" Everyone shouted.

The friends were all delighted and very grateful for Theodore. They all started singing and dancing. The youngest friend asked Charlie if she could take him home with her. Charlie smiled told the youngest friend that Theodore had to stay close to the pond where is food was.

Theodore heard all that was said and politely excused himself from the invitation. Charlie told Theodore that what he did was very brave. Theodore blushed and and slipped into the pond and swam away. He turned around for an instant and was smiling at Charlie and the friends.

It was getting late and it was a long walk back home. They all picked up their baskets and said goodbye to Theodore.

When the friends got back home the sun

was already going down. They all started gathering leafs for their beds. The friends were all exhausted from the long walk back home.

"Ouch!" shouted Charlie. "What's wrong Charlie, are you alright" Asked Chello. "It's my side again." She said while pointing to it. Chello made her lay down and rest on her leaf. "I have to make us some leaf tea." She said. Chello told her that he would make the tea instead. Chello looked at her side and noticed the bump had appeared again. The bump was bigger than before. Charlie was feeling dizzy more than before.

Chello did what he could to comfort her. He made more leaf tea and put some berries close so she could eat. One of the oldest friends saw that she wasn't getting any better, even after eating berries and drinking leaf tea. "I'll be alright Chello, don't worry." She assured him. Chello was afraid that she might be doing what she said would happen in her dream. "I'll be here if you need me Charlie." He told her. She smiled at him and then went out for a walk.

Chello tried to follow her but she insisted that he stay home. One of the oldest friends went with her on their walk and the two talked about the change that would happen soon. "It takes time, you have lots of time." He said. Charlie felt nervous inside and touched the bump on her side. She saw it growing day by day and tried to hide it from Chello.

The oldest friend and Charlie came back and it seemed like forever to Chello. They always walked together and he felt a loneliness come over him like he never felt before. "How are you feeling Charlie?" He asked her. "I'm going to be fine, don't worry about me." She answered.

The next day Charlie had noticed that the bump was gone again. She felt her side to make sure it had gone. She had lots of energy and wanted to be out with the friends. "Chello, let's do something different today" She suggested. "Like what Charlie?" He replied looking puzzled. "I want to climb up high and look out over the place where we live." She told him. Chello looked at her and thought she might be feeling ill. "I want to be up high, so I can feel what it's like to fly." She said. Chello had never heard her talk like that before.

Chello started looking for things to take with them on the climb. He found a long piece of twine. Chello thought that it might come in handy in case anything went wrong. The two of them took the twine and some berries with a basket of tea leaves.

"Let's get going Chello." Charlie told him. Both of them started walking down the path that led to the Swing. They were smiling and dancing and singing their walking song.

The sun was shining and puffy clouds filled the sky. It had turned out to be a beautiful day. The two had everything they needed for the climb that was ahead of them. Charlie asked Chello if he was happy. Chello smiled at her and said he couldn't be happier. Chello wanted to see Charlie climb up to where she could look out over where she lived. He was excited to do something he had never done before.

Soon they had arrived at the Swing. Charlie saw the grassy hill that she wanted to climb. She asked Chello if he was ready. "I couldn't be readier." He told her. He threw the twine he had brought with them over his shoulder. He gave Charlie a hug and started climbing up the grassy hill. Charlie followed after him and they made their way up to the top in no time at all.

On top of the hill there were lots of plants and tall grass growing all around. They both looked for a place to sit, while they caught their breath.

Charlie sat there looking out over the place where she lived.

"It's beautiful, you can see forever." She told Chello. "Yes it is, we are on top of the world." Replied Chello. "Where do we live Charlie?" He asked her. "We live way over there Chello." She pointed. Chello was glad to see that Charlie was doing what she wanted to do that day. He thought to himself that it was alot like her dream she talked about. Charlie always spoke of flying like a bird. Chello could never imagine what it must have been like to fly.

The wind was blowing fast over the top of the grassy hill. Chello was holding his arms out as if he had wings like a bird. Charlie was doing the same as Chello. "Look Chello, I'm flying!" She shouted. "I'm flying like a bird!" Yelled Chello. The two friends became lost in the wind, with their wings stretched out they had flown far from where they were.

Charlie and Chello spent the rest of the

day on top of the grassy hill flying to places that they never had been before.

Looking down below, they could see the friends coming to join them. Chello yelled out to them, "We're up here, high up in the sky." One of the friends looked up and saw Chello waving his arms. Charlie was standing at the edge of the grassy hill with her arms out and she was smiling from ear to ear.

"Come on up, we're having so much fun." She told them. The friends all climbed up to the top of the grassy hill and joined Charlie and Chello. They sat for awhile to catch their breath, then looked out over the whole place where they all lived. "Look over there." Said the youngest. The friends were looking over to where she was pointing. The youngest had seen the Swing. Charlie pointed in another direction and said, "That's the pond". The friends all sat on top of the grassy hill all day with Charlie and Chello looking out from on top of the

grassy hill.

Charlie showed them all how to fly, they were all having the time of their lives.

They were all so busy flying that they forgot to eat the berries they had brought with them.

"Ouch!" yelled Charlie. Chello looked over at her and was wondering what was wrong. "It's my side again." She told them. She tried to get up but it was too painful for her. Chello came over to where she was sitting and tried to make her be still. The friends saw that Charlie wasn't doing to well and went over to help her. "I will be ok, don't worry." She assured them.

The youngest friend reached into his basket and took some berries over to Charlie so she could eat. She smiled at her and started to eat the berries. Chello made some leaf tea. Chello told the friends that he would use the twine and tie it around Charlie's waist, so they could lower her down from the grassy hill.

The friends helped Chello to lowere her down. Charlie told them that she was having so much fun. When she was down from the hill, she took the twine off of her. The friends pulled it up and heard the youngest say that she wanted to go next. They all began to laugh, then tied the twine around her waist and slowly lowered her down from the top of the hill. She was laughing and smiling all the way down.

They had all finally made it down from the top of the hill. It had been a great day for all of them. It was starting to get dark, so they all decided to walk back home. Chello told Charlie that he never had so much fun before. She smiled at him and thanked him for being so smart. Chello smiled back at her and they all left to go home.

That night Charlie was feeling better and noticed that her bump was not too big. She saw that Chello was getting his

leaf ready for bed. Charlie told Chello
that she was going to sleep like this
tonight. He looked over at her and saw
that she was hanging upside down on
her leaf. Chello thought to himself that
she must have lost her mind.

  "You can't sleep like that!" He scorned
her. "Yes I can!" She snapped back at
him. Charlie thought to himself that
maybe she wasn't crazy after all.
Besides both of them had been on top of
the hill flying.

  In the morning Chello noticed that
Charlie was still hanging upside down.
He went over to her and gave her a
nudge. She just kept hanging there and
Chello nudged her again. Her eyes
popped open and said goodmorning to
her friend Chello. "How did you sleep
last night?" Asked Chello. "Oh just
fine." She replied. "You look funny!"
He told her.

  Charlie moved herself off of the leaf that
she was hanging from. "Are you going to

sleep like that from now on?" Asked
Chello. "I'm not sure Chello, maybe."
Was her answer. Chello noticed that
Charlie was looking rather pale and her
green color was changing. "How do you
feel today Charlie?" He asked her. "Not
too bad Chello." She told him.

Charlie was sitting on her leaf sipping
her tea when the friends arrived. "It's a
beautiful day!" Announced the oldest
friend. "Yes indeed it is." Replied
Charlie. The oldest friend had noticed
that her color was changing. The rest of
the friends had arrived to the leaf hut and
saw Chello trying to hang upside down
on his leaf.

"What are you doing Chello?" Asked
one of the friends. "I'm trying to feel
what it's like to fly." He replied. Charlie
knew that Chello had remembered what
she told him about the dream. Chello
wanted very badly to understand what
was happening to Charlie. He knew that
she would soon change and that he

would no longer be able to go places with her. Charlie went over to Chello and told him that the two of them would never be apart.

He thought to himself that it would be good if he could change with her.

As the days past one by one Charlie's appearance became more noticable. She looked bigger and they could hardly keep she could no longer keep up with the friends when they would go on their walks. Chello stayed close to her and made sure she didn't get too tired.

Chello was feeling sad with each passing day. Charlie tried to keep his spirits high by reminding him that they would never be apart. He asked her if she would wait for him in the sky. Charlie smiled at him and she knew that he was ok with the dream.

One day Chello came up with an idea, he was   going to make Charlie a cart so that she would not have to walk and keep up with them. The friends all laughed at him and tried not to embarrass him too much. Charlie told him it was a wonderful idea.

"Charlie where would you like to go today?" They asked her. Charlie noticed that the friends were all pooped out from pulling her around in the cart that Chello had made for her. Chello sat down trying to catch his breath then got up and went to eat some lunch. It wouldn't be long before the friends could no longer keep pulling her around with them.

Charlie prepared herself for that day to come, like she saw in her dreams. Chello made sure that Charlie had everything she needed. He would always make the leaf tea for her. He had picked fresh berries and had them hidden away for when she needed them.

The morning had come when Chello nudged Charlie to wake up and she just hung there motionless. He tried nudging her again and saw that it was no use. Sadly, he just sat on his leaf and watched *her hang until the friends came to take him away. He thought to himself how different things were that Charlie was no longer with them.*

The friends all made sure that Charlie would not be disturbed while she waited for her change.

"Chello is that you?" Whispered Charlie. Chello looked around to see who was talking to him. Chello looked around and saw Charlie hanging there and started laughing. "Chello it's me." She said. Chello couldn't believe it, Charlie was talking again. "Hi Charlie." He whispered back to her. "Can you see me Charlie?" He asked her. "No, I can't see you but I can hear you." She said to him.

Chello had found his friends and told them that Charlie could talk again. The friends all dropped what they were doing and ran to see Charlie. Charlie seemed happy as she hung there on her leaf. They all were happy and waited for her change to happen.

"Look what she's doing!" The youngest friend yelled out. The friends stood there in amazement as she started swaying back and forth on her leaf. All of a sudden she stopped swaying and Chello couldn't believe what he was seeing.

Charlie was popping out of her old skin. "Look at that!" Shouted Chello. "She's changing". Charlies new wing had appeared and it was beautiful. Her new wings were a bright orange, with blue and green. Both of her wings were finally out of her old skin. "She's beautiful!" Said the youngest friend.

Charlie had finished her change and was resting on the leaf she had been hanging from. Her old skin had dropped to the ground. Her wings were folding and unfolding, then she spoke out and asked her friends how she looked. Chello was speechless and tried to talk and the friends all told her how pretty she looked.

She smiled at them and started to lift up off the leaf she was resting on. Chello saw that she wanted to fly and was jumping up and down with delight. Charlie's wings were moving faster and faster as she began to lift higher and higher. Chello yelled out to her, "Your'e flying Charlie!" Charlie flew around the friends and then came back down to rest.

"I can't believe it!" She said to the friends. "I was flying." She told them. Chello got so excited that he became dizzy and fell to the ground. The friends all gathered around Charlie and were singing and dancing. They were all as happy as can be. It was a great day for them all.

Night had come upon them and they were all gathering their leaf beds. The stars were all shining bright that night and a shooting star could be seen forever.

The friends and Chello all looked out into the night sky and saw that each other had been tired. They slept all night next to each other.

On their way to the Swing the next day Chello and the friends sang songs and danced all the way there. Charlie flew up above them and guided them the whole way. She watched them marching along the path that she once walked on. They all looked up at Charlie fluttering over them and were so happy that she could fly.

"I see the Swing now." Said Charlie. From up above she could see places before the friends got there. As the days past the friends and Chello had grown older. Chello would be the one to change next. He would spend his afternoons pretending he could fly and wondered how long it would be before he could. Charlie stayed near him all the time.

One afternoon Chello began to feel a pinch in his side and his bump appeared the same way Charlie's did. Chello could hardly wait for his change to happen. The friends were anxious for

Chello and stayed with him every day.

Chello got bigger and bigger and the friends pulled him around in the cart he had made for Charlie. "It's happening." He said to himself. Chello climbed up to the leaf where he would hang on and wait until his change happened.

Chello had stayed there for days and Charlie would come to see him. They would talk until Chello would finally pop out of his old skin. Chello was beautiful, he had lots of blue and green with bright yellow on his wings. Chello's wings folded and unfolded and began to lift him up from his leaf. "Look at me, I'm flying!" He shouted out. "Fly like the dream Chello!" Charlie told him.

The friends were all watching and Charlie and Chello spent the rest of the day flying over all the Swing. He marveled at the way things looked from up above. "Look Chello, the pond." She showed him. "There's Theodore." Said Chello. They circled around the pond twice before they landed and came to rest on a branch.

Theodore saw that the two were new to the pond and asked them, "Do I know you?" "It's me and Chello" She mentioned. Theodore could hardly believe that it was them. Chello laughed and then Charlie started laughing. Theodore smiled at them and dipped back into the pond.

Charlie and Chello both took off again for the sky. They had lots of things to see. Chello wanted to fly over the grassy hill where they had pretended to fly.

The two were the most beautiful pair in the sky and were friends forever. All of the friends stayed close together. Theodore waited for them to come each day to the Swing. The ants had finally found a new home and the big bird was never seen again.

"Do you think old loud mouth will remember us?" Asked Chello. Charlie smiled at him and started laughing and *you can still hear her laugh to this day.*

CPSIA information can be obtained at www.ICGtesting.com
Printed in the USA
BVOW05s1406290316

442163BV00017B/86/P